THE MERLIN MYSTERY

Written by
Jonathan Gunson

Illustrated by
Marten Coombe & Jonathan Gunson

If you seek and find herein
The fabled Alchemist's Spell
Merlin's Wand is yours to keep
And all the gold as well

WARNER BOOKS

A Time Warner Company

The smoke of wizardry glimmered and sparkled in the Forest Perilous, reeling skyward from the chimney of Merlin's tumble-down and shuttered cottage.

Far above, the moon glided through a field of stars, and shafts of silver fell upon the magic realm.

'Enchanting,' whispered the shadow, watching from a leafy branch. 'It is time!'

She stole out of the forest and up the winding path, pausing at the locked cottage door. For seven centuries an unbreakable hex of silence had surrounded the house.

'Ooh, somebody … somebody at last …' The cottage trembled. 'But I mustn't … really I mustn't.'

'There …' whispered the shadow and an ambrosial gatefall spell of honeydew, treacle and sherbet shimmered radiance around the ancient portals.

'Ooh …' the cottage shuddered. 'Ooh …' it sighed. 'But, I can't … I mustn't.'

'Sugar plum?' tempted the shadow wickedly with a flicker of astral fire.

'Really I shouldn't … well, perhaps, just the one,' sighed the door, giving in, and as it creaked slowly open a shaft of bright moonlight glittered into the cottage.

★

Deep within the dreaming walls the Owl perched high in the rafters. He twitched, swaying slightly as in an odyssey of dreams he flew through a great cosmic labyrinth, hunting the mythical nine-tailed mouse.

As the night thief slid gleefully into the cottage hall, the grandfather clock spied the intruder and chimed an alarm.

'Flibbertigibbets!' quaked the waking Owl. 'Who dares invade the castle keep?'

Unseen, he floated silently down into the library, flexing his talons.

★

Nick-nacks from centuries past and future cluttered the shelves, for time knew no boundaries within the enchanted house. With spectral purpose, the shadow moved beyond the rows of spells all murmuring with magic, flowed under the astrolabe, brushed by the peacock feathers, slipped past the bottles of tinctures and apothecary jars with barely a clink, then carefully slid around the Chameleon plant with its myriad shifting colours.

Wraithlike, the intruder oozed into the library towards the velvet-shrouded reading table.

'Now!' she cried, flinging the cloth away, and reached for the prize with trembling claws; but the table was empty.

'Toads!' she hissed.

The Owl swept down out of the blackness at this moment, wings trailing spell-fire. His magic fell to earth and with a flash a Crystal Ball appeared on the table, its phosphorescent brilliance falling upon the intruder … a sleek black Cat.

'Ha …!' hooted the Owl.

The Cat shrank from the glare, peeping out from behind her claws in hissing fright.

The Owl flicked his great wingtips again, and a powerful anti-gravity spell surged out into the library. As the magic flooded over the Cat she floated helplessly up towards the rafters, slowly tumbling over and over.

Rotating majestically, the Cat floated high above the library floor with a jumble of books sailing around her.

'Who goes there?' demanded the Owl. 'A hobgoblin? A witch's cat? Or merely a cloud of soot?'

'Insolent fowl!' hissed the Cat. Her eyes seemed to grow greener and with a flash crackling black magic poured from her claws.

Gravity instantly returned and the entire contents of the library fell to the floor with a tremendous crash.

The magic roared off around the library, bringing the contents back to life. All the books began to babble and chatter, their pages fluttering.

The Owl watched in shock as the Cat landed softly beside the Crystal Ball.

'This is the wizard's,' said the Cat and drew her tail around her front paws. 'But where,' she purred to the Crystal Ball, 'is the Wand of Merlin, fabled maker of golden riches?'

'Close by,' replied the Crystal Ball, which was bursting to gossip. 'But before I tell you, first a riddle you must solve. Listen, I will tell thee … I want to tell thee:

"I paint the earth with colour bright
I frame my work with gilded light
Both rich and poor I brush with gold
As day runs out I groweth old.
Who am I?"'

The Cat had the answer in an instant.

'Wonderful!' cried the Crystal Ball. 'Now the legend of the Wand may be told.'

The Owl froze. 'No! Stop!' he cried. 'Don't ever!'

But the Cat twitched her magical whiskers and a sudden gale-force wind swept him away in a flurry of feathers across the library into a cupboard which banged tightly shut.

A phantom image of huge stones rose up above the Crystal Ball as it began to tell the legend, and cloaked figures unfurled themselves amongst the towering blocks.

'Stonehenge, seven centuries yore,' intoned the Crystal Ball. 'Dark sorcerers dreamed of ruling the world, and gathered there to plan the kingdom's destruction.'

Lightning suddenly lit the circle and a vast presence appeared looming over it, its head high in dark storm-clouds. Spell-fire blazed from a branch held in its hand and plunged into the stone ring. The giant blocks cracked and fell as a great Oak tree exploded upwards amongst them, and the cloaked figures fled in screaming panic.

'The Wizard Kell!' exclaimed the Crystal Ball. 'He came from the stars and drove the sorcerers from the kingdom with the power of the Oak branch. When the fire-battle was over, he fashioned the branch into a Wand and wrought a flaming spell-wall around the kingdom to prevent their return, creating the magic realm. Then he hid the Wand within the realm to power the spell-wall for eternity and, his work completed, returned to the stars.

'Everyday life resumed, but when autumn arrived, the leaves of the Oak tree turned to pure gold, a treasure from the stars to enrich the kingdom for ever.'

'Alchemy!' murmured the Cat excitedly.

Quercus robur

Sorbus acuparia

 As the images of golden leaves faded, the Cat gazed around.

'Where,' she hissed, 'lies this magical Wand?'

'Beyond the words of this second riddle,' replied the Crystal Ball.

> "Fine rings of magic circle me,
> A floating cosmic orb set free.
> With solar forces reaching high,
> For ever shall I roam the sky.
> Who am I?"

The Cat quickly unravelled the riddle, whereupon a jewelled music box appeared on the table.

'*Bonjour le chat,*' tinkled the box, opening its lid.

'*Enchanté,*' purred the Cat, slightly bemused.

'*You wish to see the Wand?*' said the box.

'*Oui,*' replied the Cat. '*Oui, oui!*'

The image of a tiny prince and princess rose from the music box, twirling around, and grew to life size. All around them a gorgeous ballroom appeared and a trumpet fanfare announced their arrival.

'Where is the Wand?' shouted the Cat over the noise.

'Within the story told,' replied the music box. 'Now listen carefully. Once, long after Kell's time a beautiful princess held a masked ball in the kingdom to honour her father, the king. Then just as the ball began, a gentle wizard known as Blaise appeared from the stars. He warned the king that dark sorcerers might again break into the world. This time they planned to destroy the Wand, the spell-wall and the entire magic realm.

'The king pleaded with the wizard to protect the princess, so Blaise whispered a secret name to her and tied a magic cord in her hair.'

'Safe then?' whispered the Cat.

'No,' said the music box. 'At midnight, a prince in a fabulous jewelled mask arrived with a troupe of faerie entertainers. The king was delighted and opened the spell-wall to admit them. But the players were truly a dark sorcerer and his elfin spirits in disguise.

'The sorcerer invited the princess to dance, and as they swirled around the ballroom, the faeries flew above and sprinkled lovers' black magic.

'"Oh my prince!" cried the princess, falling instantly in love with him, and in a reckless moment she untied the magic cord and let down her golden tresses.

'"Now!" shouted the sorcerer. And at once the faeries spirited her away to a dark tower in the netherworld, tying her up with the magic cord. There the sorcerer seduced her, for he needed a child with human form to enter the magic realm and find the hidden Wand. But the spell-bound princess knew nothing of this and dreamed she was living in a sunlit kingdom with her prince.

'"Soon I shall destroy the Wand and the spell-wall," the sorcerer gloated as he stood over the dreaming princess. "Then my dark forces will invade."

'Winter came, but when the child was born, the princess awoke with a shock, all alone in the cold dark tower and she wept, cradling the baby in her arms.

'Then she remembered the secret name Blaise had told her. "I will call you Merlin," she whispered. The baby opened its eyes and a crest of light appeared around its head. "Merlin, Merlin," the princess repeated. The baby sighed softly and the light grew brighter and brighter.

12

'Eventually, Blaise found the princess's tower, for which he had searched long, flying to her window disguised as a rook. But before they could flee, the dark sorcerers arrived to take the baby. Blaise quickly cast a spell and turned all the tower's door handles to molten lead, burning the sorcerers' hands.

'The enraged sorcerers set fire to the tower, and a smell of blazing timber rapidly filled the air.

'All seemed lost; then, with a flash of genius, Blaise cast a spell and threw the cord from a window. It lengthened magically to the ground and the wizard, the princess and her babe escaped down it with flames licking after them. But no sooner did they reach the ground than the dark sorcerers surrounded them.

'Blaise desperately took the cord and cast a great binding spell, hurling it around the sorcerers, who were all instantly bound into a ring of giant stones.*

'Then the wizard fled with the princess for the safety of the magic realm. The flaming spell-wall opened and the princess returned safely to the overjoyed king.

'Blaise then secretly drew the Oak Wand from its hiding place. He tied the cord around it to increase its powers and strengthen the spell-wall around the magic realm. Then, with his tasks fulfilled, he returned to the stars.'

At this moment the images faded away. The music box cheerfully shut its lid, tinkled '*Au revoir!*' and marched off to the tune of *The Marseillaise*.

And a loud crashing sounded from the library cupboard.

---

* *The ring of stone sorcerers can still be seen at Avebury in England.*

14

With a crash of splintering wood the cupboard door in the library burst open.

A regiment of toy knights in armour charged out, led by the Owl. They spied the Cat and with shouts of 'The dragon!' galloped towards the enemy.

The Cat dived quickly over the blazing embers in the fireplace and emerged in a large children's playroom. The Owl followed, and with smoking feathers landed in front of a toy castle.

In full cry the knights also jumped over the flames and headed for the castle. The leading knight, however, brought his charge to a halt, for the Cat was nowhere to be seen.

'That's uncommon strange,' he said, as the whole army pulled up in noisy confusion behind him, all banging into the back of one another, nearly knocking him off his mount. 'Dragon's fled our show of arms!' he shouted. 'Lack of bottle, what!' and a great cheer rose from the assembled company. The Cat, though rather offended, chose to stay hidden as the troops then galloped home across a tiny drawbridge into the toy castle.

★

The Crystal Ball sailed over to the Cat's hiding place.

'Madam,' said the Owl, spying the Cat, 'I shall see you off yet.'

'No you won't,' laughed the Cat and she blinked a spell of warfare.

The castle fired off its cannons in little puffs of smoke at the Owl who, with a squawk, fled to the rafters.

'I love castles, don't you?' chimed the Crystal Ball.

'Love? Adore!' cried the Cat. 'Great places for hiding Wands don't you think?'

She purred and rubbed her cheek on the Ball.

'Indeed,' it agreed. 'Let me show you.'

Images of heraldic flags and dragons rose from the toy castle, swirling into the air to the sound of heralds' trumpets.

'Once Merlin was grown, 'twas a time of turmoil,' said the Crystal Ball. 'The royal Pendragon family arose with King Uther, Queen Igraine and their great castles of Tintagel and Terribil. 'Twas a time when Arthur, the royal son, grew to manhood, drew a magic sword from a stone and became king of the magic realm.

'Merlin built Castle Camelot and a round table for Arthur, with questing knights, tournaments and golden pavilions in the sun … a shining moment! A fantastic moment when time stood still as Merlin called upon all the great magic of the cosmos and completed the Wand with the symbols of the Pendragon, the flaming spell-wall, and his own mystical Crystal Ball.

'The Wand's powers of alchemy were infinitely increased, and thereafter the wealth of the realm grew and grew, seven centuries after Kell's magic Oak branch saved the kingdom.'

As the Cat watched the scene wide-eyed, the Owl dropped unnoticed from the rafters in a hunter's dive, talons outstretched.

'Tally ho!'

The wind screamed through his feathers as he dived at the Cat, down, down …

Aesculus hippocastanum

Fraxinus excelsior

Swoosh! The Owl's talons swept towards the Cat and grabbed … nothing.

The Cat had pressed against a secret wall panel that gave way to a flight of stone stairs. She plunged down, with the Crystal Ball flying after her.

Soon she found herself in a vaulted crypt steeped with moonlit stained-glass beauty. A tomb over-laid with an effigy of King Uther Pendragon for ever sleeping lay before them.

'Perhaps here the Wand of Alchemy also lies sleeping,' whispered the Cat and the sound echoed around the stone pillars.

'Sleeping … sleeping … sleeping.'

'Just the Wand?' said the Crystal Ball. 'But alchemy needs all three cosmic forces. The Alchemist's Spell, the Wand and the Stone.'

'Stone?' puzzled the Cat. 'What stone?'

'The Philosopher's Stone,' intoned the Crystal Ball. 'The ancient, secret, incomprehensible, heavenly, blessed and triune universal Stone of the sages. It is the force the Wand uses to transmute base metals into gold. 'Tis awakened and with us now.'

'Here?' said the Cat, excited.

The Crystal Ball hovered and spoke. 'It lies betwixt the words of this riddle:

"I'm seen by all but none may touch
I'm new but old and wander much.
I'm silver not, though silver seem
I'm known for making lovers dream
Who am I?"'

As the Cat bathed in the luminous colours pouring through the stained-glass window, she whispered the answer. Instantly, in a cloud of astral fire, a carved stone figure of a king with a broken sword appeared, set perfectly in a stone arbour.

'Arthur,' whispered the Crystal Ball. 'His sword, once drawn from the stone, now broken in battle.'

Starlight shimmered again and a second stone figure appeared beside Arthur. A beautiful, ethereal figure holding a sword with the legend EXCALIBUR on its blade.

'The lady of the lake … Nimue!' gasped the Cat.

'You know of the water sprite princess?' asked the Crystal Ball.

'In another life …' replied the Cat wistfully. 'She rose from the waters of Lake Avalon and brought Arthur the fabled sword as a symbol of loyalty from the faerie kingdom. The gift gave her right of passage through the spell-wall.'

At that moment a third figure appeared.

'Merlin, and the Wand!' hissed the Cat. Then her momentary excitement faded. 'But only of stone.'

'Nimue became Merlin's apprentice,' whispered the Crystal Ball. 'To this day she lives in the Forest Perilous and the woodsmen say she is a witch. Merlin teaches her the natural magic of the trees, but never will he teach her the Alchemist's Spell, nor show her the Wand of Merlin.'

A shadow suddenly flickered across the stone columns as the Owl came gliding softly into the crypt.

'Sulphur sublime!' he rasped.

This time there was no escape for the Cat. A fiery alchemical symbol appeared on the floor of the crypt, and a flagstone swung open.

The Cat and the Crystal Ball dropped into the blackness, down, down …

Landing with a crash on a stack of dried lavender, the Cat found herself in a darkened laboratory full of glowing apparatus. She shivered as a familiar voice whispered in her mind.

'Hurry!' it hissed, then faded away.

'What is this place?' she whispered to the Crystal Ball.

'The place of alchemy,' said the Owl, suddenly appearing right beside her ear.

The Cat sprang back, ready for another battle of spells.

'Shall we call a truce,' sighed the Owl, 'without further fisticuffs?'

'Show me the Wand then,' ventured the Cat warily.

'In spirit,' said the Owl, 'then you must leave.'

He bowed his head and a brilliant image of the Wand appeared. Light shone across its mystical surfaces and reflections shimmered in its crystal sphere.

'Alchemy!' commanded the Owl, and a stream of gold poured from the Wand.

'But this is nothing,' he said, seeing the Cat's amazement, 'compared with the Pendragon Alchemy.'

'The Pendragon Alchemy?' said the Cat. 'I know not of this.'

''Tis the greatest alchemy,' said the Owl, his eyes gleaming. 'It began when Arthur drew the sword from the stone and turned away from the quest for gold. He took instead the path of his dream, to lead and care for his people.

'But on this path the very riches he had turned from poured in from all over the realm. This is the Pendragon Alchemy, whence comes the greatest wealth of all.'

The Cat seemed fascinated by this, but as the Owl gazed at the Wand, she secretly prepared to attack.

Hovering tantalisingly close, the Wand continued to pour out gold. Like quicksilver, the Cat leapt. But the Wand vanished in a puff of stardust.

'Vampires and wishbones!' swore the Cat. 'You promised.' She glared at the Owl.

'I said *in spirit*,' replied the Owl evenly.

'Cheat,' hissed the Cat.

'Really?' puffed the Owl, bridling. 'Then unravel this riddle and the Wand is yours.'

As the Owl began, the Cat seemed to listen closely, but her tail lashed and flicked as she secretly forged an '*off with his head*' hex.

'"The fabled Wand of Alchemy
In Uther's realm now veiled by sea
Outside and in with castled view
At once on earth and under true.

'Tis far beneath the shining dream
Of sun and moon, or starlight's gleam
Yet when these orbs shed tears of gold
Each mirrored splash it sees unfold.

Where lies the Wand of Merlin?"'

Though as clever as Christopher, the Cat could not decipher this.

'Deceiver!' she spat, and launched the potent hex she had been forging. 'Swindler, dodger, humbug!'

But the Owl ducked and the energy bolt roared past him, crashing into the centuries of collected spells piled to overflowing around the laboratory shelves. The colliding magic exploded and raged out through the cottage walls into the surrounding forest.

The sun rose, changed its mind and set again. Autumn, winter, spring and summer flooded the enchanted glades in a moment;

birds awoke in a chorus of song and millions of flowers burst upwards.

★

A cloud of spell-fire also suddenly swirled around the Cat with nebulae, stars and supernovae erupting in a universe of celestial fireworks. Then in a moment she was gone, and in her place stood a young woman of unearthly beauty, her eyes flashing. She grabbed hold of the Owl.

'Where is Merlin?' she cried.

'Nimue!' gasped the Owl.

'There is great danger,' said Nimue. 'The dark sorcerers approach. They intend to take the Wand by force, but I know not where they will strike.' She trembled then repeated, 'Where is Merlin?'

'How did you get here?' demanded the amazed Owl.

'I shape-shifted into a cat so that the sorcerers would not recognize me,' said Nimue. 'Then I came to save the Wand … and Merlin.'

She let go of the Owl, then suddenly broke down, weeping with frustration. 'Please, I must see him.'

'Why?' continued the Owl, unconvinced.

'Because, you featherhead,' interrupted the Crystal Ball who suddenly understood, 'she loves him.'

'Loves … him?' choked the Owl.

'Will you help me?' said Nimue with a secret smile. Gently she smoothed the ancient bird's ruffled feathers. 'There's not much time.'

The Owl spread his wings and spell-fire spiralled around him. In a moment he, too, vanished in an astral blaze. In his place stood a tall, powerful figure.

The wizard of the Forest Perilous.

'Merlin!' gasped Nimue.

For a silent moment, the two magical beings faced each other.

'You know,' began Merlin, 'I've always …'

'Yes?' whispered Nimue.

'Go on, go on,' said the Crystal Ball encouragingly.

'That is to say,' he tried again. 'Ever since you and I … I've always …'

'Oh, he's hopeless,' said the Crystal Ball to the enchantress. 'He's absolutely over the moon about you too!'

Nimue burst into laughter and the lovers fell into each other's arms.

'We shall fight these sorcerers together with the great magic,' said Merlin once he had recovered sufficiently. 'We shall fight them on the hills, and in the valleys, we shall never surrender!'

'But I know nothing of the great magic, Lord Merlin,' said Nimue.

'Then I shall teach you,' he cried excitedly. 'Come on!'

He snapped his fingers and in a flash they were back in the library.

★

The wizard gazed into the fireplace. There was so much to say.

'Once,' he said, 'when I was very young, my mother took me to a castle by the sea.'

'Your mother, the princess, was she very beautiful?' said Nimue, watching him closely.

'I dream of her still,' said Merlin sadly. 'We built sandcastles, and there was a wonderful cave. We could go right through one side and out the other.'

'The sea-cave at Tintagel Castle!' cried Nimue. Her eyes suddenly widened. 'The Wand is hidden there?'

'Indeed,' said Merlin, 'and it must be protected from the sorcerers. We shall travel at dawn.'

'And the Alchemy Spell?' asked Nimue. 'Does it, too, lie within the cave?'

Merlin laughed and threw a handful of herbs into the fire. Above the fireplace, blue light suddenly flickered around a still-life painting. He reached in, drew forth a large spell-book and opened it.

Magic flared from the pages as he taught her the Spell of Alchemy and Blaise's binding spell.

'The Spell of Alchemy,' said Merlin. 'Cast it once and the Wand appears. Twice and the alchemy takes hold.'

He scattered more herbs and golden blooms floated from another painting.

'Marigolds,' she said breathlessly. 'My friends of the fields.'

Fragrance filled the library as Merlin gently placed one in her hair. Within moments, many more appeared around it.

'What does this mean?' she said.

'Each soul's purpose is different,' he said, 'and each must find that purpose. Yours is a caring for the natural world, which rewards you in kind.'

He watched as the flowers continued to multiply.

'This is the Pendragon Alchemy.'

'That's quite enough hocus pocus for one day,' said the spell-book, rustling its pages.

The wizard and the enchantress smiled at each other as Merlin blew the candles out, and the spell-book floated back into the painting.

★

At midnight, Nimue stood alone with her secrets and stared out of a window. She shivered as, far off, lightning flickered and the mysterious unseen voice whispered again.

'Hurry!' it hissed urgently.

Citrus limon

The smoke of wizardry glimmered faintly in the darkened Forest Perilous, drifting from the chimney of Merlin's cottage. The door opened and Nimue slipped away with a large and very ancient book gliding behind her. In the doorway something shiny paused, then covertly followed as she disappeared into the trees.

★

Some hours later, and far away, as dawn's first light caught the ramparts of Tintagel Castle, a faint glow appeared in the sea-cave below.

Deep in the cavern, unseen voices echoed from the rocky walls.

'Hurry … hurry!' they whispered urgently.

Nimue cast herbs onto her lantern flame, and recited the Alchemist's Spell from Merlin's grimoire. A deep, resonant tone filled the cave, building to a thunderous roar. Crackling streams of light poured from the walls and with a flash the Wand of Merlin appeared. The sound faded away and Nimue gasped as the exquisite object slowly and silently rotated in the air before her, rainbow-coloured shivers of magic flickering around its glittering surfaces. The Wand itself was far more beautiful than the ghostly image she had seen in the alchemy laboratory.

Trembling, she reached out, and as soon as she touched it, a ripple of magic flowed out to the cave walls.

The walls bulged and cracks started to appear in the rock. Suddenly a hand shot out, then an arm, and a head. At last, he stood there, the dark sorcerer, a ghostly and malevolent figure, and an acrid smell like burning pitch filled the cave.

34

With a soft ringing sound, the Crystal Ball suddenly appeared beside Nimue.

'Surprise!' it said.

'Shssh!' whispered Nimue. 'What are you doing here?'

'Incurable curiosity,' the Crystal Ball replied, then suddenly shuddered as it caught sight of the sorcerer.

'Oooh, he looks a mean one, who's he?'

'A dark sorcerer,' said Nimue. 'He's going to care for the world.'

'Caring? A dark sorcerer caring?' The Crystal Ball shivered, incredulous.

'We have an arrangement,' said Nimue. 'He desires something from the magic realm. I agreed to bring it to him and he granted me the power of human form so that I could leave my life as a water sprite and walk abroad in the world for ever. He forged the magic sword Excalibur to prove his good intentions and I brought it into the kingdom through the lake for the once and future king, Arthur Pendragon.'

'So you have been working for the sorcerer all along,' said the Crystal Ball, aghast. 'What does he want in return?'

'The Alchemist's Spell,' whispered Nimue. 'And the Wand of Merlin.'

'The Wand?' said the Crystal Ball, shocked. 'The sorcerer could destroy it and the spell-wall too.'

'Welcome, daughter of darkness,' said the sorcerer, and the sound of a million waiting sorcerers echoed from the far-off netherworld.

'He looks like a really bad apple,' whispered the Crystal Ball in fright.

'Release us and give me the Wand,' said the sorcerer.

'No!' cried the Crystal Ball. 'Don't you see, he's going to…'

Black magic darted from the sorcerer's fingers, and the Ball shattered into tinkling pieces on the cave floor.

36

For a moment that seemed to last an eternity, Nimue looked at the broken Crystal Ball.

She suddenly saw that her dream of life in the magic realm was everything the sorcerers planned to destroy. She thought of their false promises, and how she had deceived Merlin while he taught her the great magic.

'I stay with the realm,' she announced.

'Fool!' hissed the sorcerer. 'Release us and give me the Wand or lose everything.'

But as he spoke, a marigold flower fell from her hair. In the sorcerer's malevolent presence the bloom shrivelled to blackness and the enchantress knew what she must do.

Nimue made as if to close the spell-book, but instead secretly turned up the black page of Blaise's binding spell. She smiled and lofted the Wand as if to give it to the sorcerer.

'Yes!' he cried.

Instead Nimue shouted the powerful incantation:

'Deadly nightshade shall ye see,
'Tis end of time and alchemy!'

Magic exploded from the Wand and raged towards the sorcerer.

Just at that moment, Merlin appeared in the cave. Fearing that Nimue was about to release the dark sorcerer into the magic realm, he leapt directly into the line of fire. Too late, she fought to hold back the spell, and the fiery bolt struck him with all its cosmic power.

The light of ages past and future blazed from Merlin's eyes as the great magic of Blaise's binding spell crashed into him.

In a desperate attempt to fight off the deadly force he called up every powerful hex and spell he had ever learned. In his heart, though, he knew it was hopeless, for the great magic was unbreakable. But still he fought to the end.

Nimue fell back as images of Camelot, Excalibur, King Arthur, Blaise, Kell, Stonehenge and a blizzard of gold-dust swirled around Merlin faster and faster until the maelstrom of time and history flew out of control. Then in a flash, he disappeared into the cave walls, leaving behind a spiral of fading energy.

Laughing in triumph, the dark sorcerer advanced towards Nimue and the Wand. Then his face was etched with fear as the potent energy began to tear at him as well. Bolts of lightning poured out from the Wand and wrapped around him in a deadly embrace. With a cry of rage he stabbed his clawed fingers at Nimue and a shower of sparks fell around her.

'No longer,' he cried, 'shall you have the power …'

Then he too was swept away, and the cave returned to silent rock and stone.

★

Chattering bird calls and a hundred forest sounds filled the cave as the Wand floated from Nimue's hands and was drawn back into the cave walls.

The spell-book turned into tumbling leaves, releasing all its magical wildlife spells. Seagulls soared out of the cave above the castle into streaming sunlight, screeching with joy, for the magic realm was safe again from the sorcerers.

★

As her hair turned to glistening rivers, though, Nimue wept, and with those tears her change back into a water sprite gathered pace. Within moments, she was part of the neverending waves lapping the beach.

★

Merlin's laughter suddenly rolled around the cave. From the waves, Nimue could see her lover's face shimmering in the rocky headland.

'I meant to save us,' she cried. 'Is it too late?'

'Neither you nor I can bring us back,' said Merlin, 'but the Pendragon Alchemy can.'

'Yes?' she said, hope soaring.

'A great quest shall begin,' he said. 'The Spell of Alchemy will be found by a seeker who follows the Pendragon Alchemy. It lies waiting, hidden within this legend.'

Merlin laughed again, looking at the sky full of gulls.

'Why are you laughing?' she asked.

'Because we, too, are alive!' he said. 'The spell has bound us together as the cave and the sea. We shall always be together as keepers of the Wand … until the seeker finds the Spell.'

'And then?' she said.

Quercus robur

'The seeker will cast the Spell and the Wand will appear,' he whispered. 'Then we too shall return.'

'To walk abroad in the magic realm?' she said.

'Together,' he smiled.

Suddenly, a brilliant ringing sound came from the cave.

The Crystal Ball reassembled itself to shining perfection and appeared in the sea-swept entrance.

'*Enchanté, au revoir!*' it sang, and sailed off over the castle ramparts into the sky to play with the gulls.

'Merlin … Merlin,' whispered Nimue.

As the tide ebbed, her voice faded away.

★

To this day, the wizard and his enchantress can be heard whispering in the enchanted cave below the crumbling ramparts of Castle Tintagel in Cornwall. Strangers from all corners of the Earth come to listen to the magic as every day Nimue appears, in her water spirit form as the wild or gentle waves sweeping the edges of Merlin's sea-cave.

★

At high tide for a magical time the lovers talk and laugh under Tintagel's stormy ramparts, then depart to return and meet again and again, awaiting the Pendragon Alchemy …

… and the seeker.

Ulmus procera

The Legend of Merlin's Wand

Long ago, the great Wand was created to protect the world from evil. The wizard Merlin instilled the Wand with powerful magic, called the Pendragon Alchemy.

Thirty-six inches (ninety centimetres) in length, the Wand is believed to be the most powerful magical object ever to exist. Lost for millennia, it has waited for a seeker wise and true of purpose to discover the Alchemist's Spell and set it free.

The head of the Wand is made from ancient gold-threaded Brazilian crystal, set into silver pendragons with a gilded staff representing a branch from the Tree of Life. A gold ring of flames surrounds the crystal, representing the spell-wall protecting the kingdom. The ring is inset with symbols of the seven metals of alchemy: lead, iron, tin, copper, mercury, silver and gold. Entwined around the branch is the magic cord used by the wizard Blaise to turn dark sorcerers to stone. The gilded cord draws all the magical powers towards the tip of the Wand.

The Alchemist's bracelet

The enchanted bracelet of gold alchemy symbols. Infused with alchemical magic, the bracelet was drawn around the wizard's arm when casting the Alchemist's Spell. The twelve symbols contain the secret ingredients for creating gold: mercury, *aqua fortis*, copper, fire, iron, air, tin, earth, lead, water, sulphur and salt.

THE REVERSE SIDE OF THE WAND

The three wizards' symbols appear in a firmament of solid silver stars. Kell is represented by the Sun, Blaise by the Moon, and Merlin by Saturn.

The wizards' collective power is also enhanced with the symbols sculpted in gilded bronze.

THE ALCHEMIST'S KEY

The sublimate of sulphur symbol, key to alchemy and master of all the golden alchemy symbols. A shard of precious lapis lazuli enhances the key's alchemical powers.

MERLIN'S CHEST OF SANCTUARY

Made from solid oak by Merlin to protect the Wand, the chest is sealed with three magical locks, which can be opened only with the ancient spell-keys of the three wizards.

THE GOLDEN VIAL

The Alchemist's glass vial of pure 24 carat gold drawn from the River Nile. The vial produces an endless stream of gold when a wizard casts the Spell.

For William Wallace

'We were very young when we first visited the cave. The sound of the sea rolled by outside and seemed to fill the cavern with whispering voices. It was then that all the magic he had taught me took hold.'

This puzzle has been validated by Mensa, the international society for people of high intelligence. For membership information contact: British Mensa, St John's Square, Wolverhampton WV2 4AH, United Kingdom. E-mail: mensa@dial.pipex.com (for UK and Irish Republic). American Mensa, 1229 Corporate Drive West, Arlington, Texas 76006-6103 USA. E-mail: AmericanMensa@compuserve.com (for USA). Or contact the Mensa website at http://www.mensa.org

Thanks to Fortnum & Mason and Selfridges & Co. for permission to reproduce their clocks

HOW TO ENTER
THE MERLIN MYSTERY

The answer to *The Merlin Mystery* is the Alchemist's Spell, and the method of casting it. Draw these two elements of the Spell, separately, on a piece of paper and place your answer, along with your name, address and telephone number, in a sealed envelope. In the top left-hand corner of the envelope draw the final word of the Spell as a picture. Then send your entry by post/mail to The Merlin Mystery, PO Box 1803, London NW1 8NQ, United Kingdom.

By entering *The Merlin Mystery* all entrants will be deemed to have accepted and be bound by these rules and conditions of entry:

1. *The Merlin Mystery* is open to everyone except employees and their families of HarperCollins*Publishers* Ltd, their associate publishers, advertising and promotions agencies and printers.

2. Entries will only be accepted by post/mail to The Merlin Mystery, PO Box 1803, London NW1 8NQ, United Kingdom.

3. Entries will be accepted prior to but not opened until January 1, 1999. Entries received prior to January 1, 1999 will be marked with the date and time the entry was received and opened on or after January 1, 1999 in the same order as the entries were received according to the date and time marked on the entry. The date of the first correct entry will be determined by the date of its postmark. In addition, you may register your name and contact number on the official *Merlin Mystery* website (**www.merlinmystery.com**) along with the date and time when you posted/mailed your entry.

4. Responsibility will not be accepted for entries lost, damaged, delayed or mislaid in the post/mail or offered for delivery insufficiently stamped or incorrectly addressed. Proof of posting/mailing will not be accepted as proof of delivery; neither will registering your details with the *Merlin Mystery* website. Entries which are altered, illegible or not in accordance with these rules will be disqualified.

5. Entries will be judged by the authors, who alone know the solution to the puzzle. The judges' decision will be final and no correspondence can be entered into. The winner will be the first correct entry as determined by the postmark and the time the entry was received. Any entry not received within 2 weeks of its postmark shall be deemed disqualified under paragraph 4. The winner will be the first correct entry received by HarperCollins in accordance with paragraph 3 and opened after January 1, 1999. The winner must not only have the correct solution, but also be able to satisfy the judges as to the process whereby he or she has reached that solution. Do **not** include the explanation as to how you solved the puzzle with your entry. If your entry is correct you will be contacted by HarperCollins and asked to explain the means by which you solved the puzzle.

6. There is no minimum age for entrants, but those under the age of 16 should seek permission from their parent or legal guardian to enter.

7. *The Merlin Mystery* will run until the correct solution is received (but no earlier than January 1, 1999) or until December 31, 2001 (the closing date), whichever is the sooner.

8. The winner will be notified by HarperCollins by telephone or by post/mail within 10 days of his or her selection. By accepting the prize, the winner grants to HarperCollins, their associate publishers and advertising and promotions agencies the right to use the winner's name and likeness for the purposes of advertising and promotion and to participate in the award ceremony without further permission or additional compensation, except where prohibited by law.

9. In the unlikely event of two or more correct entries arriving at the same time, a skill-based tie-breaker will come into effect.

10. The solution to the puzzle will be kept on an encrypted disk in the vaults of the Bank of England.

11. The solution will be published once the puzzle has either been solved or the closing date has expired. If the puzzle remains unsolved, the Wand will be auctioned, and the proceeds thus raised, along with the cash prize fund, will be donated to the World Wildlife Fund, Panda House, Weyside Park, Godalming, Surrey GU7 1XR, UK, reg. charity no. 201707.

12. The winner will win Merlin's Wand (approximate retail value $25,000) (for which no cash or alternative prize will be offered); and the cash prize fund. The cash prize fund for US residents is set at $125,000. The winner will be responsible for any taxes on the prizes. After the winner is announced, their name and home town will be available to anyone writing to HarperCollins*Publishers*, enclosing a self-addressed, stamped envelope by December 31, 2001 to HarperCollins*Publishers*, 77-85 Fulham Palace Road, London W6 8JB, UK. No information will be sent until after the winner's selection or December 31, 2001, whichever is the sooner.

13. All entries received become the property of HarperCollins*Publishers* Ltd and cannot be returned. By entering, entrants grant to HarperCollins, their associate publishers and advertising and promotion agencies the right to edit, publish, promote and otherwise use their entries without notice or compensation. It will not be possible to acknowledge receipt of entries.

14. HarperCollins shall have complete discretion over the interpretation of the rules and conditions and reserve the right to refuse to award the prize to anyone in breach of the rules and conditions.

15. Entry into *The Merlin Mystery* is governed by the laws of England. It is void in the US states of FL, MD, VT, and ND and wherever else prohibited by law.